THE ELSON READERS

BOOK ONE
(REVISION OF ELSON PRIMARY SCHOOL READER, BOOK ONE)

BY

WILLIAM H. ELSON
AUTHOR ELSON GOOD ENGLISH SERIES

AND

LURA E. RUNKEL
PRINCIPAL HOWE SCHOOL, SUPERIOR, WISCONSIN

SCOTT, FORESMAN AND COMPANY
CHICAGO   NEW YORK

1-R

For permission to adapt copyrighted material, grateful
acknowledgment is made to *The Youth's Companion* for
"The Go-to-Sleep Story" by Eudora Bumstead; to
Kindergarten and First Grade for "Bobbie's Yellow
Chicken," from "The Little Brown Hen," and for "The
Parade on Washington's Birthday," from "Their Flag,"
both by Carolyn S. Bailey; to *The Outlook* for "The
Mouse, the Cricket, and the Bee" by Sidney Dayre, and
for "Thanksgiving in the Hen-House" by Frances M.
Fox; to Milton Bradley Company for "The Pine Tree
and Its Needles" by Frances M. Fox, from *For the Chil-
dren's Hour;* and to Alfred F. Loomis for "The Little
Rooster," by Charles Battell Loomis.

CONTENTS

3

PREFACE

In preparing Book One of the *Elson Readers*, the authors have taken great care to make the transition from the Primer natural and easy. The selections, notably those in the early pages, are alike simple and kindred in theme with those of the Primer; similarly, the first three stories are based on the "oral background" plan followed throughout the Primer. Moreover, in the earlier part of this book each page tells a distinct unit of the story-plot. As the child gains in ability to get thought from the printed story, the help afforded by page unity and by the oral background of familiarity with the unfolding plot is gradually withdrawn.

The stories and poems throughout the book represent the best to be found in child-literature, and include a wide variety, thus appealing to many phases of child-interest and supplying material suited to the varied needs of the school. There are stories not only from the past — fables and folk tales — but also present-day stories, rich in ideals of home and country and of helpfulness to others — ideals to which the World War has given new meaning that the school-reader should perpetuate.

This book is distinctive for the large amount of reading matter that it contains, as well as for the care with which the 425 words of the text are distributed. Simplicity of vocabulary and sentence structure characterizes the book throughout.

Some of the stories of Book One are presented in dramatized form, while many others lend themselves admirably to this treatment, thus offering project material of an excellent type. The many action stories particularly adapt this book to the purposes of silent reading, a project of another important kind.

5

All the pretty things put by,

Wait upon the children's eye,

Sheep and shepherds, trees and crooks,

In the picture story-books.

—*Robert Louis Stevenson.*

LITTLE GUSTAVA

Once there was a little girl.

Her name was Gustava.

One day she heard a little bird.

It sang and sang and sang.

"Oh, spring has come!" said Gustava.

"Mother, do you hear the bird?

I am so happy! I love the spring."

Her mother gave her some bread and milk.

She sat in the warm sun to eat it.

Little Gray Kitten saw her there.

She ran to Gustava.

"Mew, mew," said the kitten.

"What have you to eat?"

"I have bread and milk," said Gustava.

"Will you have some?

I will give you some of my good milk."

"Mew, mew," said Gray Kitten.

"It is good. Give me some more."

"Oh, I am so happy," said Gustava.

"Spring is here, Gray Kitten."

"I like spring, too," said Gray Kitten.

Soon little Brown Hen came by.

"Good day, Brown Hen," said Gustava.

"I am glad to see you.

Here is some bread for you.

Eat all you want.

Spring is here, Brown Hen.

Are you not glad?

I am so glad that winter is over.

Do take some more bread."

"Cluck, cluck," said little Brown Hen.

"Spring makes me happy, too."

"Coo, coo; coo, coo," said the doves.

"Oh, I hear my white doves," said Gustava.

They flew down to her.

"I am so glad to see you," she said.

"How pretty your white wings are!

Winter is over, White Doves.

Now you can find food.

But I will give you some bread today."

She threw them some bread.

"Oh, spring has come," said Gustava.

"We are all so happy."

"We like spring, too," said the doves.

Soon her little dog came by.

"Bow-wow, bow-wow," he said.

"Don't you want me, too?"

"Oh, yes, Little Dog," said Gustava.

"You must have some food, too.

Spring is here, Little Dog.

We are so glad that winter is over.

Take some of this milk.

I have not had any yet.

But take all you want.

I will put it on the floor for you.

I like to see you eat."

Then Gustava sat down on the floor.

Little Dog, Gray Kitten, Brown Hen, and the White Doves sat around her.

Just then her mother came out.

"Oh, Gustava!" she said. "You have no dinner.

I will get you some more bread and milk."

"I gave it all away," said Gustava. "Spring made me so happy."

—*Adapted from Poem by Celia Thaxter.*

WHO TOOK THE BIRD'S NEST?

"Tweet-tweet, tweet-tweet!" said Yellow Bird.

"I made a pretty little nest.

I made it in the little tree.

I put four eggs in it.

Then I flew to the brook.

How happy I was!

But now I can not find my nest.

What shall I do? What shall I do?

I will see if White Cow took it."

"Tweet-tweet, tweet-tweet!" said Yellow Bird.
"White Cow, did you take away my nest?"
"Oh, no!" said White Cow. "Not I!
I did not take away your nest.
I would not do such a thing.
I gave you some hay for your nest.
I saw you put your nest in the little tree.
You sang and sang and sang.
It was a beautiful little nest.
I am sorry you can not find it.
But I did not take it," said White Cow.
"Oh, no! I would not do such a thing."

"Tweet-tweet, tweet-tweet!" said Yellow Bird.

"Who took my little nest?

Oh! Here comes Brown Dog.

Brown Dog, did you take away my nest?

I put it in the little tree.

There were four eggs in it."

"Oh, no!" said Brown Dog.   "Not I!

I would not do such a thing.

I gave you some hairs for your nest.

I am sorry you can not find it.

But I did not take it. Oh, no!

I would never do such a thing!"

"Tweet-tweet, tweet-tweet!" said Yellow Bird.

"Who took my little nest?

Oh! Here comes Black Sheep.

Black Sheep, did you take away my nest?

I put it in the little tree.

Then I flew to the brook."

"Oh, no!" said Black Sheep.   "Not I.

I would never do such a thing.

I gave you wool to make your nest soft.

It was the prettiest nest I ever saw.

Oh, no!   I did not take it away.

I would never do such a thing."

"Moo, moo!" said White Cow.

"Bow-wow!" said Brown Dog.

"Baa, baa," said Black Sheep.

"Who took Yellow Bird's nest?

We think a little boy took it.

We wish we could find him."

A little boy heard them.

He hung his head.

Then he ran into the house and hid behind the bed.

He would not eat his dinner.

Can you guess why?

The little boy felt very sorry.

Soon he came out of the house again.

He took the nest back to the little tree.

"Dear Yellow Bird," he said, "I am sorry.

I took your nest from the little tree.

But I will never do such a thing again."

"Tweet-tweet, tweet-tweet, tweet-tweet!"
sang Yellow Bird.

"I am as happy as can be."

—*Adapted from Poem by Lydia Maria Child.*

THE MOUSE, THE CRICKET, AND THE BEE

Once there was a little mouse.

One spring day she sat in the sun.

A cricket and a bee came along.

"Winter is over," said the little mouse.

"Let us make a house.

We are so little.

We can all live in one little house.

We can be so happy there."

"That is a good plan," said the cricket.

"I like that plan, too," said the bee.

"Where shall we make a house?" said the bee.

"Let us find a very dark place," said the cricket.

"I like the dark.

It is dark under the barn.

The sun can not find us there.

I like to chirp in the dark.

I do not like the light."

"Oh, dear! Oh, dear!" said the mouse.

"I do not like to live in the dark.

I am not happy in the dark.

The warm sun is the place for me.

Let us try to find a light place."

"Yes, yes!" said the bee. "Yes, yes!
I like the sunshine, too.
I know a good place for a house.
It is up in a tall tree.
It is very light there.
The tree is in a pretty meadow.
The meadow has flowers in it.
The sun will keep us warm.
The wind will sing to us.
I like to buzz in the sunshine.
I am very happy in the sunshine."

"Oh, dear! Oh, dear!" said the cricket.

"I never chirp in the sunshine, and
I can not fly.

I can not live in a tall tree.

Oh, dear, no! That place would not do
for me.

What shall I do? What shall I do?"

"Let us try my place," said the mouse.

"I know a good place for a house.

It is on the ground.

It is in the sunshine, too.

I like to live in a corn field.

We can eat the corn.

We can run and play in the sunshine.

That will be such fun.

I can make a warm home for us.

There we can be very happy."

"Oh, dear! Oh, dear!" said the bee.

"I can not eat corn.

That place would not do for me.

We can not live together."

So the bee flew to the tall tree.

"Buzz, buzz," he sang in the sunshine.

"See how high I am.

My home is best."

The cricket ran under the barn.

"Chirp, chirp," he sang in the dark.

"I have a good hiding place.

My home is best."

The mouse ran into the field.

She made a soft, warm nest.

"Squeak, squeak," she said in the corn.

"My home is best."

She went to sleep in the sunshine.

—*Adapted from Poem by Sidney Dayre.*

BOBBIE'S YELLOW CHICKEN

Bobbie's grandmother lived on a farm.

One summer he went to see her.

He saw many cows and sheep there.

He saw many horses and pigs, too.

Bobbie lived on the farm all summer.

He was as happy as he could be.

One day he said, "Grandmother, I wish
I could live here always.

I have great fun here."

One day Grandmother went to the barn.

Bobbie went with her.

She said, "See this little yellow chicken, Bobbie."

"May I have her?" said Bobbie.

"She is the prettiest chicken I ever saw."

"Yes, Bobbie," said Grandmother.

"You may have her.

You must give her food every day.

Some day she will lay an egg for you."

Bobbie gave her food all summer.

She grew and grew and grew.

One day Grandmother said, "Bobbie, your mother wants you to come home.

You may come again next summer."

Bobbie felt sorry to leave the farm.

He went to the barn.

"Good-bye, little yellow chicken," he said.

"I must go home to mother.

Please do not forget me.

I will see you again next summer."

"I will not forget you, Bobbie," said the little yellow chicken.

"When you come back I will lay an egg for you."

Bobbie went home to his mother.

His mother was waiting for him.

How glad she was to see him!

Bobbie was glad to see her, too.

"Oh, Mother!" he cried, "Grandmother gave me a little yellow chicken.

I gave it food and water every day.

It is my own little chicken.

Next summer it will lay big white eggs for me.

Do you think it will know me when I go back?"

The next summer Bobbie went back to Grandmother's.

He ran at once to the barn.

He looked and looked and looked, but he could not see his little chicken.

Just then he saw a big brown hen jump off her nest.

Grandmother laughed. "There is your little yellow chicken," she said.

"You did not know her when you saw her."

"Oh, see the egg in her nest!" said Bobbie.

"I did not know my little yellow chicken.

But she did not forget to lay an egg for me."

How proud the big brown hen was!

—Carolyn S. Bailey—Adapted.

From *Kindergarten and First Grade,* Milton Bradley Co.

THE GO-TO-SLEEP STORY

"I must go to bed," said little dog Penny.

"But first I must say good night to Baby Ray.

He is kind to me.

He gives me some of his bread and milk.

I will see if he is asleep."

So little dog Penny found Baby Ray.

His mother was telling him a Go-to-Sleep story.

Little dog Penny heard it.

This is what he heard,

The doggie that was given him to keep,
    keep, keep,
Went to see if Baby Ray was asleep,
    sleep, sleep.

"We must go to bed, too," said the two kittens.

"But first we must say good night to Baby Ray.

He gives us milk for our dinner.

Let us see if he is asleep."

So the little kittens found Baby Ray.

They heard the Go-to-Sleep story.

This is what they heard,

One doggie that was given him to keep, keep, keep,

Two cunning little kitty-cats, creep, creep, creep,

Went to see if Baby Ray was asleep, sleep, sleep.

"We must go to bed, too," said the three bunnies.

"But first we must say good night to Baby Ray.

He gives us green leaves for our dinner.

Let us see if he is asleep."

So the bunnies found Baby Ray.

They heard the Go-to-Sleep story.

This is what they heard,

One doggie that was given him
    to keep, keep, keep,
Two cunning little kitty-cats, creep,
    creep, creep,
Three pretty little bunnies with
    a leap, leap, leap,
Went to see if Baby Ray was asleep,
    sleep, sleep.

"We must go to bed," said the four white geese.

"But first we must say good night to Baby Ray. He gives us corn. Let us see if he is asleep."

So the four geese found Baby Ray. They heard the Go-to-Sleep story. This is what they heard,

One doggie that was given him
    to keep, keep, keep,
Two cunning little kitty-cats, creep,
    creep, creep,
Three pretty little bunnies with
    a leap, leap, leap,
Four geese from a duck-pond, deep,
    deep, deep,
Went to see if Baby Ray was asleep,
    sleep, sleep.

32

"We must go to bed," said the five little
chicks.

"But first we must say good night
to Baby Ray.

He gives us bread.

Let us see if he is asleep."

So the five little chicks found Baby Ray.

He was just going to sleep.

They heard all of the Go-to-Sleep story.

This is what they heard,
One doggie that was given him to keep,
keep, keep,
Two cunning little kitty-cats, creep, creep,
creep,
Three pretty little bunnies, with a leap,
leap, leap,
Four geese from the duck-pond, deep,
deep, deep,
Five downy little chicks, crying peep,
peep, peep,
All saw that Baby Ray was asleep, sleep,
sleep.

—*Eudora Bumstead—Adapted.*

A LULLABY

Lullaby, oh, lullaby!

Flowers are closed and lambs are sleeping;

Lullaby, oh, lullaby!

Stars are up; the moon is peeping;

Lullaby, oh, lullaby!

Sleep, my baby, fall a-sleeping,

Lullaby, oh, lullaby!

—*Christina G. Rossetti.*

THE ANT AND THE DOVE

"I want some water," an ant once said.

"I will go to the brook.

I can get some water there."

So she went to the brook.

But she tumbled into the water.

"Help! Help!" she cried.

"The water is cold!"

A dove heard the ant.

"I will help you!" cried the dove.

So she threw a leaf into the brook.

The ant got on the leaf.

"Ooo-oo-o-o!" blew the wind.

It blew the leaf to the land.

Then the ant got off the leaf.

"Thank you, kind dove," she said.

"Sometime I will help you."

Soon a man came by.

He saw the pretty dove.

He said, "I will catch her."

So he kept very still.

He came very near to the dove.

"Coo, coo!" said the pretty dove.

She did not see the man.

But the ant saw him.

She said, "I will help the good dove."

So she bit the man and made him jump.

The man cried out, "Oh! Oh!"

Then the dove saw the man.

Away she flew!

She was safe, and the ant was happy.

—*Retold from a Fable by Æsop.*

THE PROUD LEAVES

A big tree grew in a meadow.

Green leaves grew on the tree.

One day they said to the sun,

"How beautiful we are!

We make the tree beautiful.

What would the tree be if it had no leaves?

We make a cool shade, too.

Boys and girls play in our shade.

They swing and laugh and sing.

All the birds fly into the tree.

They sing to us,

'Tweet-tweet, tweet-tweet.'

See their little nests all around us!

The wind sings through us.

It says, 'Oo-oo-o-o! oo-oo-o-o! oo-oo-o-o!'"

So the leaves felt very proud.

All at once they heard a soft little voice far below. It said, "Leaves, we help the tree, too."

"Who are you?" said the leaves.

"We are the roots," said the voice. "We get food for you.

You are beautiful, but you die. New leaves come every spring. But we live on and on.

If we should die, the great tree would die, too."

The leaves said, "You do help the tree, kind roots.

We will not forget you again." —*A Russian Fable.*

39

THE DOG AND HIS SHADOW

Once there was a big dog.

When he got a bone he always hid it.

He never gave a bit to any other dog.

If he saw a little dog with a bone he
would say,

"Bow-wow! Give me that bone!"

Then he would take the bone.

One day he took a bone from a little dog.

"The little dog shall not find this bone,"
he said. "I will take it far away.

I will go across the brook and hide it."

So the big dog ran to the brook.

There was a little bridge over the brook.

The dog ran out on the bridge.

He looked down into the water and thought he saw another dog there.

He thought the dog had a bone, too.

"I will take that bone," said the big dog.

"Then I shall have two bones.

Bow-wow! Bow-wow!" said the big dog.

Then his own bone fell out of his mouth.

It fell into the brook.

The big dog could not get it out.

There was no dog in the water at all!

The big dog had seen his own shadow.

—Retold from a Fable by Æsop.

THE KITE AND THE BUTTERFLY

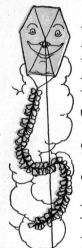

A kite flew far up into the clouds.

It played with the wind.

It looked at the sun.

The kite saw a butterfly far below.

"Look at me!" said the kite.

"See how high I am!

I can see far, far away.

Maybe I shall fly to the sun.

Don't you wish you were a kite?

Then you could fly with me."

"Oh, no!" said the butterfly.

"I do not fly very high.

But I go where I please.

You fly very high.

But you are tied to a string!"

—*A Russian Fable.*

THE CAT AND THE FOX

One day a cat met a fox in the woods.

They were looking for food.

The cat wanted a fat mouse.

The fox wanted a fat rabbit.

They had looked and looked.

But all the fat rabbits and all the fat mice were hiding.

The fox was very cross.

When he wanted a rabbit, he wanted it!

The cat was not cross at all.

When she wanted a mouse, she could wait for it.

She said, "Good morning, Mr. Fox.

I am glad to see you.

How are you getting on?"

The fox looked at the cat and laughed.

"You foolish little cat!" he said.

"I can always get along all right.

I know so many tricks.

How many tricks do you know?"

"I know just one trick," said the cat.

"Ha, ha!" laughed the fox.

"Just one little trick! What is that?"

"I can jump up into a tree," said the cat.

"When the dogs come — jump! I am safe!"

"Ha, ha!" laughed the fox.

"Just one little trick!

I know many tricks. They are all better than your trick, too.

Let me tell you some of them.

Then the dogs will never catch you."

"All right!" said the cat.

Just then they heard a great noise.

It was a hunter on his horse.

His dogs were running and barking.

Jump! The cat was safe in a tree!

But the dogs got Mr. Fox!

"I am just a foolish
little cat," said the cat.

"I know only one trick.

But one trick is sometimes
better than many."

—*Retold from a Fable by Æsop.*

45

A WISH

May: Oh, see the pretty birds!
How fast they fly!
They look so happy.
I wish I had wings.
Then I could fly, too.
But I have only legs.
My legs are short, and
they are slow, too.
Wings can go fast.
When I go home I must
walk.
It will take me a long time.
I must go through the meadow.
Then there is such a hill to go up!
I do not like to go up high hills.
Oh, if I were only a bird!
How fast I would fly home to mother!

46

Bird: Are you sure you would like to be a bird?

I eat worms for my dinner.

May: Oh, dear! I did not think of that!

I should not like to eat worms.

I like bread and milk for my dinner.

Bird: Would you like to sleep up in a tree?

My little ones like a tree-top bed.

May: Oh, no! That would not do at all!

The wind sometimes shakes the tree.

It would shake me out of the nest.

My little white bed is best for me.

Bird: What would you do when the hawk came?

My little birds hide from the hawk.

May: I am so big the hawk would see me.

Oh, I am so glad I am not a bird!

It is best for me to be a girl.

MOLLY AND THE PAIL OF MILK

Molly lived on a farm.

A little cow lived on the farm, too.

The cow gave good milk.

One day Molly's mother said, "You may have this pail of milk, Molly.

Go to town and sell it.

You may have all the money you get."

"Oh, thank you, mother!" said Molly.

She put the pail of milk on her head and walked down the road.

"When I sell this milk, I shall get some money," she said.

"Then I will buy some eggs.

I will put the eggs under our hens.

The hens will sit on the eggs.

Soon little chickens will be hatched.

I will sell the chickens.

With the money I will buy more eggs.

I will buy many, many eggs.

Soon I shall have many little chickens.

They will grow big and fat.

I will sell them all.

What shall I do with all that money?

Oh, I know! I will buy some geese.

Then I will buy some ducks.

I will buy a pig.

I will buy a horse.

I will buy a cow.

I will buy a farm.

I will build a little house on the farm.

I will live in the little house.

How happy I shall be there!

This little pail of milk will do it all."

It made Molly happy just to think of it.

She began to jump and sing.

Down came the pail of milk!

Poor Molly! She did not sell the milk.

She could not buy any eggs.

She could not buy ducks and geese, a pig, a horse, a cow, and a little farm.

She could not build a little house.

She counted her chickens too soon.

Next time she will wait until they are hatched.

—Retold from a Fable by Æsop.

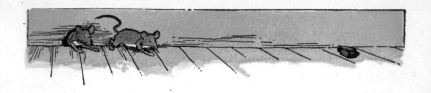

THE FINE PLAN

Once some mice lived in a big house.

They ran all over the house.

Patter, patter, patter, went their feet!

The house was full of mice.

A cat lived in the big house, too.

He was a big cat.

He liked to catch the mice.

He caught some every day.

The mice were afraid of him.

They said, "What shall we do?

This big cat will catch us all.

He will eat us up.

Oh, what shall we do?"

"I know what to do," said a little mouse.

"The cat makes no noise when he walks.

We can not hear him.

I have a fine plan.

We must hang a bell on his neck!

The bell will make a noise.

Ting-a-ling! ting-a-ling! it will go.

We shall hear the bell.   Then we
shall know that the cat is coming.

We will run away.

The cat can not catch us."

"What a fine plan!" said
the other mice.

"Yes! yes!   The cat must
have a bell on his neck!

Then he can not catch us."

The mice jumped for joy.

The little mouse was very proud.

"How wise I am!" he said.

"Now we shall be safe."

But Old Gray Mouse laughed.

He was wiser than the little mouse.

"Ha, ha!" he laughed, "ha, ha, ha!

That is a fine plan, little mouse.

But who will hang the bell
on the cat?

Will you, little mouse?"

"Oh, no, no! He would eat me up!"

But someone must put the bell on the cat!

The little mouse had not thought of that.

He ran away as fast as he could go.

He cried "Squeak! squeak!" all the way

home.
—*Retold from a Fable by Æsop.*

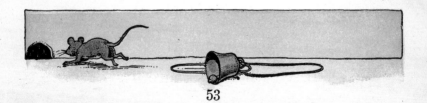

THE RACE

One day a little hare was in a meadow.

A little tortoise was there, too.

He was creeping to the river for a swim.

"How slow you are!" said the hare.

"You can not hop. You can only creep.

Look at me! See how fast I hop!"

And the little hare gave a great hop.

"I am slow," said the tortoise.

"But I am sure.

Would you like to run a race with **me**?"

"Run a race!" cried the hare.

"How foolish that would be!

I hop and you creep.

How can we run a race?"

"Let us try," said the tortoise.

"Let us race to the river.

We shall see who gets there first."

"The river is a long way off," said the hare.

"But I shall soon be there.   Good-bye!"

Off went the little hare, hop! hop! hop!

Off went the tortoise, creep, creep, creep.

Soon the hare was nearly to the river.

It was a warm day.

"I will rest a little," he said.

So the hare rested and ate some leaves.

Then he felt sleepy.

"It is very warm," he said.

"I will sleep a little.

That foolish old tortoise is slow.

I shall wake up before he creeps here.

Then I can hop to the river.

I shall be there long before he comes."

So the little hare went to sleep.

The little tortoise came creeping on.

He did not stop to eat.

He did not stop to sleep.

He went on and on, creep, creep, creep.

By and by he came to the river.

The little hare slept a long time.

Then he waked up with a jump.

"Dear me! I must hop along," he said.

"Where can that slow tortoise be?

He is not here yet."

The little hare hopped
on to the river.

There was the little
tortoise waiting for him!

"Creep and creep

Beats hop and sleep!"
said the tortoise.

—*Retold from a Fable by Æsop.*

THE COCK AND THE FOX

One morning a cock flew to the top of a barn.

He flapped his wings and called, "Cock-a-doodle-doo!"

Now a fox heard the cock.

So he came to the barn.

He wanted to get the cock and eat him.

But the fox could not reach him.

So he called up to the cock,
"Come down, friend!
Have you heard the news?
The beasts and the birds are
going to live together.
They will not hurt each other
any more.
They will not eat each other up.
They will all be friends.
Come down, friend cock!
Let us talk about the news."
But the cock knew the fox
had many tricks.

So he stayed on top of the barn.

He looked far, far away.

"What do I see? What do I see?" said he.

"Well, what do you see?" asked the fox.

The cock looked far, far away.

"Oh! the dogs are coming! The dogs are coming!" he said.

The fox got up in great haste.

"Good-bye," he said. "I must go!"

"Oh, no, friend," said the cock. "Don't go. The dogs won't hurt you, will they?

You said the beasts and the birds were going to live together and be friends.

Let us talk about the great news."

"No, no! I must run away," said the fox.

"Maybe the dogs have not heard the news."

So he ran off as fast as he could go.

That time the cock was wiser than the fox.

—Retold from a Fable by Æsop.

THANKSGIVING IN THE HEN-HOUSE

Brown Hen: This is Thanksgiving Day.
How cold it is!
It has snowed all day.

Gray Goose: Indeed it has.
I do not like this day at all.
I wish Jack would come.
It is time for our dinner.
Maybe he will forget us today.

Little Chick: Peep, peep, I am hungry, too.
All the little chicks are hungry.

Red Cock: Cheer up, Brown Hen.

Cheer up, Gray Goose.

Cheer up, Little Chick.

This is Thanksgiving Day.

We must all be happy today.

Brown Hen: We can not be happy, Red Cock,
when we are hungry.

We want some water, too.

We don't like to eat snow.

Gray Goose: How cold it is outside!

Red Cock: But it is warm in here.

Jack has filled all the cracks
to keep us warm.

The wind can not hurt us now.

And the fox can not get us.

I am hungry, too, but I won't
be sad today.

This is the best day of the year.

Big Turkey: Red Cock, you are right.

Brown Hen and Gray Goose are too cross.

We should all be happy today.

Red Cock: Let us sing a glad Thanksgiving song.

Will you sing first, Brown Hen?

You have a fine voice.

Brown Hen: Cut—cut—ca--da—cut!

Red Cock: Now let us all sing together.

Sing loud.

There! That is fine.

Mother: What a noise in the hen-house!
The poor chickens want their
Thanksgiving dinner.

Father: Jack, you forgot them!
Take them some food.

Jack: Yes, indeed I will.
I will give them a basket of corn
and wheat.

Molly: And I will take them some water.
Poor chickens! They have not had
any Thanksgiving dinner.
Let us run to the hen-house.

Gray Goose: Here come Jack and Molly. Jack has a basket of corn and wheat.

Brown Hen: And Molly is bringing a pail of water, too.

Red Cock: Hurrah! I guess the children liked our Thanksgiving song. Let us all sing again. One, two, three, sing!

Jack: How happy they all are in the hen-house this evening!

Molly: They like Thanksgiving Day, too.

—*Frances M. Fox.*

THE CHRISTMAS FAIRY

It was the day before Christmas.

Two little children went to the woods.

They wanted to find a Christmas tree.

Poor little children! They had never had a Christmas tree.

"Oh, dear!" said the little girl.

"We have nothing to put on the tree."

"We must find a tree with many cones on it," said the little boy.

"Cones will make our tree beautiful."

"Yes, yes!" said the little girl.

"We must find a tree with cones on it."

1-R

The children walked on and on.

But they could not find a tree with cones on it.

By and by night came.

The children were very, very tired.

They could not find their way home.

So they sat down to rest.

Soon the little girl fell asleep.

The little boy was tired, too, but he did not close his eyes.

"I must take care of sister," he said.

"I will put my coat around her to keep her warm."

He sat there a long time until he shook with the cold.

By and by he saw a very bright light.

It waked his little sister.

Soon the children saw a beautiful fairy.

She came right up to them.

"Who are you?" asked the little boy.

"I am the Christmas Fairy," said the fairy.

"I am always in the woods at Christmas time.

I make the woods bright at night.

Then good little boys and girls can find the prettiest trees.

Come, children! I will take you to a beautiful tree."

The fairy took them to a beautiful tree.

It had many, many cones on it.

"Here is your tree," said the fairy.

Then she said, "Little cones, light the tree."

The little cones began to shine like gold.

"Oh, what a wonderful Christmas tree!" said the children.

"It will light you all the way home," said the fairy.

"It will shine for you on Christmas Day, too."

The children took the beautiful tree.

It lighted them all the way home.

They were very, very happy.

—Edna V. Riddleberger.

BABY'S STOCKING

Hang up the baby's stocking,
Be sure you don't forget.
The dear little baby darling
Has never seen Christmas yet.

Write, "This is the baby's stocking
That hangs in the corner here.
You have never seen her, Santa,
For she only came this year.

But she is the prettiest baby!
And now before you go,
Just fill her stocking with goodies
From the top way down to the toe."

THE BIG MAN AND THE LITTLE BIRDS

One day a tall man went for a ride.

He was going along a country road.

Some friends were with him.

Near the road was an apple tree.

He saw two little baby birds in the road.

They had just tumbled out of their nest in the apple tree.

The mother bird was flying about, near them.

But she could not put them into the nest.

"Tweet-tweet, tweet-tweet!" she cried.

She wanted the men to help her.

70

"Let us help the bird," said the tall man.

"No, we can not stop," said his friends.

But the tall man jumped from his horse.

He put the little birds back into the nest.

"Tweet-tweet, tweet-tweet!" said the mother bird.

She was trying to thank the man.

Then the tall man jumped up on his horse.

He soon caught up with his friends.

"I had to help the bird," he said.

"I could not have slept tonight if I had not helped her."

The tall man was named Abraham Lincoln.

OUR FLAG

There are many flags in many lands,
    There are flags of every hue,
But there is no flag in any land
    Like our own Red, White, and Blue.

Then "Hurrah for the Flag!" our country's
    flag,
  Its stripes and white stars, too;
There is no flag in any land
  Like our own Red, White, and Blue.

—Mary Howliston.

AMERICA

(To be memorized)

My country, 'tis of thee,
Sweet land of Liberty,
  Of thee I sing;
Land where my fathers died,
Land of the pilgrims' pride;
From every mountain side
  Let Freedom ring.

—Samuel Smith.

THE PARADE ON WASHINGTON'S BIRTHDAY*

Grandfather and Grandmother had a flag.

It was an old, old flag.

It was nearly as old as Father.

They gave the flag to Father.

He loved the old flag.

Patty and Ned loved it, too.

They hung it out of the window every Flag Day.

One day Father said, "There will be a parade on George Washington's Birthday.

It will be a fine parade.

I will take Patty and Ned to see it."

"That will be great fun," said Ned.

The children jumped for joy.

"Hurrah! hurrah!" they cried.

---

*Adapted from "Their Flag," in *Kindergarten and First Grade*, used by permission of Milton Bradley Co.

The great day came at last.

But Father could not take Ned and Patty
to the parade.

Their Grandmother was sick.

Father and Mother had to go to see her.

Patty and Ned felt very sad.

But they did not cry.   Oh, no!

Patty said, "We can not see the parade.

But we can hang our flag out of the
window."

"Yes," said Ned.   "Father and Mother
would like us to do that."

So they hung the flag out of the window.

Soon they heard a great noise.

"Oh, it is the parade!" said Ned.

"It is coming down our street.

I am so glad our flag is out."

The parade went right by the house.

Every one saw the old, old flag.

They said, "Hurrah for the old, old flag!"

Patty and Ned felt very proud.

Soon Father and Mother came home.

Patty and Ned told them about the parade.

"Oh! we had a wonderful day!" said Patty.

"Hurrah for the old, old flag!" said Ned.

"Hurrah for George Washington!" said

Father.
—Carolyn S. Bailey—Adapted.

THE LITTLE RED HEN

A little red hen once found a grain of wheat.

"Who will plant this wheat?" she asked.

"I won't," said the dog.

"I won't," said the cat.

"I won't," said the pig.

"I won't," said the turkey.

"Then I will," said the little red hen. "Cluck! cluck!"

So she planted the grain of wheat.

Soon the wheat began to grow.

By and by it grew tall and ripe.

"Who will reap this wheat?" asked the little red hen.

"I won't," said the dog.

"I won't," said the cat.

"I won't," said the pig.

"I won't," said the turkey.

"I will, then," said the little red hen. "Cluck! cluck!"

So she reaped the wheat.

"Who will thresh this wheat?" said the little red hen.

"I won't," said the dog.

"I won't," said the cat.

"I won't," said the pig.

"I won't," said the turkey.

"I will, then," said the little red hen. "Cluck! cluck!"

So she threshed the wheat.

"Who will take this wheat to the mill to have it ground?" asked the little red hen.

"I won't," said the dog.

"I won't," said the cat.

"I won't," said the pig.

"I won't," said the turkey.

"I will, then," said the little red hen. "Cluck! cluck!"

So she took the wheat to the mill.

By and by she came back with the flour.

"Who will bake a loaf of bread with this flour?" asked the little red hen.

"I won't," said the dog, the cat, the pig, and the turkey.

"I will, then," said the little red hen. "Cluck! cluck!"

So she baked a loaf of bread with the flour.

"Who will eat this bread?" asked the little red hen.

"I will," said the dog.

"I will," said the cat.

"I will," said the pig.

"I will," said the turkey.

"No, you won't," said the little red hen. "My little chicks and I are going to do that. Cluck! cluck!"

So she called her four little chicks, and they ate up the loaf of bread.

—*Old Tale.*

THE LOST EGG

Bobbie had a pretty hen named Brownie.

Brownie had a soft nest in the barn.

Can you guess why she sat there so long?

There were ten white eggs under her.

By and by Brownie heard a "Peep-peep!"

The shells of the eggs were breaking.

Little chicks were coming out of the shells.

Soon Brownie had nine little chicks.

She kept them under her wings, where it was warm.

"Peep, peep, peep!" said the nine chicks.

"Where is my other chick?" said Brownie.

"I had ten eggs. I see only nine chicks."

"Cluck-cluck, cluck-cluck," said Brownie to her little chickens.

"Let us take a walk."

She took them into the garden, to find Bobbie and his mother.

"Oh, Mother," cried Bobbie, "look at Brownie's little chicks!"

"How many has she?" asked his mother.

"I will count them," said Bobbie.

"One, two, three, four, five, six, seven, eight, nine. There are nine little chickens."

"Why, Bobbie!" said his mother, "she had ten eggs. Where is the other chicken?"

Then his mother counted them.

She counted nine chickens, too.

"I will run to the barn," said Bobbie. "I may find it there."

Away he ran as fast as he could go.

There was the egg, right in the nest!

Bobbie took it up to look at it.

But the egg fell to the ground.

Hark! What did he hear?

"Peep-peep! Peep-peep!"

He looked at the egg and saw
a big crack in the shell.

Then Bobbie saw another
little chicken.

He gave it to Brownie, and
she put it under her wing.

All the other little
chickens ran about and
flapped their wings.

They were so happy!

Brownie was happy, too. She had found
the lost chick.

—*Norse Folk Tale.*

THE GOATS IN THE TURNIP FIELD

Once a boy had three fine goats.

Every morning he took them to the hill so that they could eat the green grass.

The goats were very happy on the hill.

When evening came, the boy would take them home.

Once they ran into a turnip field.

The boy could not get them out.

What do you think he did?

He sat down and cried.

Along came a rabbit, hop, hop, hop.

"Why are you crying?" asked the rabbit.

"Oh, oh! I can not get my goats out of the turnip field," said the boy.

"I will do it for you," said the rabbit.

So he ran after the goats.

But he could not get them out.

Then the rabbit sat down and cried.

Soon a fox came along.

"Rabbit, why are you crying?" asked the fox.

"I cry because the boy cries," he said.

"The boy cries because he can not get his goats out of the turnip field."

"I will do it for him," said the fox.

So the fox ran after the goats.

But he could not get them out.

Then the fox sat down and cried.

As they were crying, a wolf came by.

"Fox, why are you crying?" said the wolf.

"I cry because the rabbit cries," said the fox.

"The rabbit cries because the boy cries.

The boy cries because he can not get his goats out of the turnip field."

"I will do it for him," said the wolf.

So the wolf ran after the goats.

But he could not get them out.

Then the wolf sat down and cried, too.

A little bee saw them all crying.

"Wolf, why are you crying?" said the bee.

"I cry because the fox cries," said the wolf.

"The fox cries because the rabbit cries.

The rabbit cries because the boy cries.

The boy cries because he can not get his goats out of the turnip field."

"I will do it for him," said the bee.

Then they all stopped crying and began to laugh. "Ha, ha! Ha, ha, ha!" they said.

"How can a little bee like you do it?"

But the bee flew into the turnip field.

He flew right to a big goat's back.

"Buzz-z-z!" he said, and out the goats ran!

Do you know why they ran out so fast?

They ran all the way home, too.

The boy laughed and ran after them.

—*Norwegian Folk Tale.*

THE KIND CRANES

Six hungry little birds once sat by the sea.

"Let us cross the sea," said one.

"We can get fat worms over there."

"But the sea is so wide!" said another. "How can we get across?"

Soon a fish came along.

"Fish, will you take us across the sea?" asked the little birds.

"I will take you down into the sea!" said the fish.

"We will go just like this!"

And he swam down, down, down, into the sea.

"Dear! dear!" said the little birds.

"Dear! dear! Let us wait."

So the hungry little birds waited.

By and by a sheep came walking along.

"Sheep, will you take us across the sea?" asked the little birds.

"I never swim," said the sheep, "and I can not fly.

Why don't you wait for the cranes?"

"Who are they?" asked the little birds.

"They are great, big birds," said the sheep.

"Their wings are so strong that they can fly across the sea.

They have long beaks and long necks.

They have long legs and big backs.

The cranes are very kind.

Every year they take other little birds across the sea.

They will take you, too."

So the hungry little birds waited.

By and by four cranes came flying along.

The little birds called to the first crane,
"Will you take us across the sea?

We can get some fat worms over there."

"My back is full of little birds now,"
said the first crane. "Ask the last crane.

He can take you across."

So the little birds called to the last crane,
"Will you take us across the sea?"

"Yes, I will take you," he said.

"My back is nearly full.

See all the little birds on it!

But you are so little that I can find a
place for you. Hop on!"

The six little birds hopped on to his back.

The other birds made a place for them.

"Are you all right?" asked the crane.

"Here we go, little birds."

The little birds held on with their beaks and their claws.

Away they flew, across the wide, wide sea.

They found all the worms they could eat.

And the six little birds got fatter and fatter.

—*Old Tale.*

THE NORTH WIND

"The North Wind is cold,"
 The Robins say;
"And that is the reason
 We fly away."

"The North Wind is cold;
 He is coming, hark!
I must haste away,"
 Says the Meadow Lark.

"The North Wind is cold
　And brings the snow,"
Says Jenny Wren,
　"And I must go."

"The North Wind is cold
　As cold can be,
But I'm not afraid,"
　Says the Chick-a-dee.

So the Chick-a-dee stays
　And sees the snow,
And likes to hear
　The North Wind blow.

—*Rebecca B. Foresman.*

WHAT DOES LITTLE BIRDIE SAY?

What does little birdie say,
In her nest at peep of day?
Let me fly, says little birdie,
Mother, let me fly away.

Birdie, rest a little longer,
Till the little wings are stronger.
So she rests a little longer;
Then she flies away.

What does little baby say,
In her bed at peep of day?
Baby says, like little birdie,
Let me rise and fly away.

Baby, sleep a little longer,
Till the little limbs are stronger.
If she sleeps a little longer,
Baby too shall fly away.

—Alfred, Lord Tennyson.

THE HEN AND THE SQUIRREL

One day a hen met a squirrel.

"Friend Hen," said the squirrel, "do you see that tall oak tree?

It is full of good acorns.

Let us get some to eat."

"All right, friend Squirrel," said the hen.

So they ran to the tree.

The squirrel ran right up the tree and ate an acorn.

"How good it is!" he said.

The hen tried to fly up and get an acorn.

But she could not fly so high.

So she called up to the squirrel,

"Friend Squirrel, give me an acorn."

The squirrel found a big acorn.

He threw it down to her.

The acorn hit the hen, and cut her head.

So she ran to an old woman and said,

"Old Woman, please give me a soft cloth.

Then I can tie up my poor

head."

"First give me two hairs,"
said the old woman.

"Then I will give you
a soft cloth."

The hen ran to a dog.

"Good Dog, give me two hairs," she said.

"I will give them to the old woman.

The old woman will give me a soft cloth.

Then I can tie up my poor head."

"First give me some bread," said the dog.

"Then I will give you two hairs."

The hen went to a baker and said,

"Oh, Good Baker, give me some bread.

I will give the bread to the dog.

The dog will give me two hairs.

I will give the hairs to the old woman.

The old woman will give me a soft cloth.

Then I can tie up my poor head."

"First get me some wood," said the baker.

"Then I will give you some bread."

The hen went to the forest and said,

"Oh, Good Forest, give me some wood.

I will give the wood to the baker.

The baker will give me some bread.

I will give the bread to the dog.

The dog will give me two hairs.

I will give the hairs to the old woman.

The old woman will give me
a soft cloth.

Then I can tie up my head."

"First give me some water,"
said the forest.

"Then I will give you wood."

The hen went to a brook.

"Brook, give me some water.

I will give it to the forest.

The forest will give me wood.

I will give the wood to the baker.

The baker will give me bread.

I will give the bread to the dog.

The dog will give me two hairs.

I will give them to the old woman.

The old woman will give me a
soft cloth.

Then I can tie up my head."

The brook gave the hen water.

She gave the water to the forest.

The forest gave her some wood.

She gave the wood to the baker.

The baker gave her some bread.

She gave the bread to the dog.

The dog gave her two hairs.

She gave the two hairs to the old woman.

The old woman gave her a soft cloth.

So the hen tied up her poor head.

—*Old Tale.*

THE PINE TREE AND ITS NEEDLES

A little pine tree lived in the woods.

It had leaves like long green needles.

But the little pine tree was not happy.

"I do not like my green needles," it said.

"I wish I had beautiful leaves.

How happy I should be if I only had gold leaves!"

Night came.

Then the Fairy of the Trees walked in the woods.

"Little pine tree," she said, "you may have your wish."

In the morning the little pine tree had leaves of gold.

"How beautiful I am!" it said.

"See how I shine in the sun!

Now I am happy!"

101

Night came.

Then a man walked in the woods.

He took all the gold leaves and
put them into a bag.

The little tree had no leaves at all.

"What shall I do?" it said.

"I do not want gold leaves again.

I wish I had glass leaves.

Glass leaves would shine in the sun, too.

And no one would take glass leaves."

Night came.

The Fairy walked in the woods again.

"Little pine tree," she said, "you may have
your wish."

In the morning the tree had glass leaves.

"How beautiful I am!" it said.

"See how I shine in the sun!

Now I am happy."

Night came.

Then the wind came through the woods.

Oh, how it blew!

It broke all the beautiful glass leaves.

"What shall I do now?" said the tree.

"I do not want glass leaves again.

The oak tree has big green leaves.

I wish I had big green leaves, too."

Night came.

Then the Fairy of the Trees walked in the woods again.

"Little pine tree," she said, "you may have your wish."

In the morning the little pine tree had big green leaves.

"How beautiful I am!" it said.

"Now I am like the other trees.

At last I am happy."

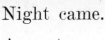

Night came.

A goat came through the woods.

He ate all the big green leaves.

"What shall I do?" said the tree.

"A man took my leaves of gold.

The wind broke my leaves of glass.

A goat ate my big green leaves.

I wish I had my long needles again."

Night came.

The Fairy walked in the woods again.

"Little pine tree," she said,

"you may have your wish."

In the morning the little pine
tree had its long needles again.

"Now I am happy," said the tree.

"I do not want any other leaves.

Little pine needles are best
for little pine trees."

—*Old Tale.*

104

HOW GOSLING LEARNED TO SWIM

One day Little Gosling went into a pond.

"Why do you go into the pond?"
asked the chicken.

"I am going to learn to swim,"
said Little Gosling.

"Then I will peep," said the chicken.

So the chicken peeped.

"Why do you peep?" asked the duckling.

"Little Gosling swims, so I peep,"
said the chicken.

"Then I will quack," said the
duckling. So the duckling quacked.

"Why do you quack?" asked the rabbit.

"Little Gosling swims, the chicken
peeps, so I quack," said the duckling.

"Then I will leap," said the rabbit.

So the rabbit leaped.

"Why do you leap?" asked the black colt.

"Little Gosling swims, the chicken peeps,

The duckling quacks, so I leap,"
said the rabbit.

"Then I will run," said the black
colt. So the black colt ran.

"Why do you run?" asked the
white dove.

"Little Gosling swims, the chicken peeps,

The duckling quacks and the rabbit **leaps,**

So I run," said the black colt.

"Then I will coo," said the white
dove. So the white dove cooed.

"Why do you coo?" asked the brown dog.

"Little Gosling swims, the chicken peeps,

The duckling quacks and the
rabbit leaps,

The black colt runs, so I coo,"
said the white dove.

"Then I will bark," said the brown dog.

So the brown dog barked.

"Why do you bark?" said the yellow calf.

"Little Gosling swims, the chicken peeps,

The duckling quacks and the rabbit leaps,

The black colt runs and the white dove coos,

So I bark," said the brown dog.

"Then I will moo," said the yellow calf.

So Little Gosling swam and the chicken peeped,

The duckling quacked and the rabbit leaped,

The black colt ran and the white dove cooed,

The brown dog barked and the yellow calf mooed.

And Little Gosling learned to swim.

—*English Folk Tale.*

I DON'T CARE

I

A horse and a brown colt once lived in a meadow.

One day the gate was open.

"I will run out of the gate," said the brown colt.

"No, no!" said the horse.

"You must stay in the meadow."

"Why?" asked the brown colt.

"I do not know," said the horse.

"But the old white horse told me to stay. So I shall stay."

"I don't care!" said the colt.

"I do not like it here.

If I run down the road, I shall have more fun."

So off he ran, down the road.

By and by he met the old white horse.

"Why are you here?" asked the old horse.

"I want some fun," said the colt.

"I am tired of staying in the meadow."

"The meadow is the best place for you," said the old white horse.

"You are safe in the meadow.

You are too little to see the world."

"I don't care!" said the brown colt.

He shook his head and ran on.

By and by he met a mule.

The mule was pulling a big cart.

"Why are you here?" he asked the colt.

"You should be in the meadow.

The town is close by, and it is no place for a little colt like you."

"I don't care! I want some fun," said the brown colt.

II

The colt ran on until he came to the town.

He had never seen a town before.

What a noise the carts made!

The little colt was frightened.

He wanted to run back to the meadow.

Then some men and boys ran after him.

They shouted at him and tried to catch him.

Soon he came to a big glass window.

He saw his shadow in the window, and he thought it was another colt.

"Oh, there is another colt just like me!" said the little brown colt.

"I will ask him the way to the meadow."

But it was not another colt.

It was only his shadow he saw in the glass.

The little brown colt ran into the window and broke the glass.

The glass cut him, and he fell down.

Then some men caught him.

They took the little colt back to the meadow and shut him in.

Now he does not want to run away.

He never says, "I don't care" any more.

—*Gertrude Sellon.*

THE CAMEL AND THE PIG

I

One day a camel and a pig were talking.

The camel was proud because he was tall.

But the pig was proud because he was short.

"Just look at me!" said the camel.

"See how tall I am!

It is better to be tall, like me."

"Oh, no!" said the pig.

"Just look at me!

See how short I am!

It is better to be short, like me."

"If I am not right, I will give up my hump," said the camel.

"If I am not right, I will give up my snout," said the pig.

Soon they came to a garden.

All around it was a wall.

There was no gate in the wall.

The camel was so tall that he could see over the wall. He could see fine, ripe fruit in the garden.

His neck was so long that he could reach over the wall and get the fruit.

He ate all he wanted.

But the poor pig was short.

He could not reach over the wall.

He could not get inside, because there was no gate.

"Ha, ha, ha!" laughed the camel.

"Now would you rather be tall or short?"

II

Soon they came to another garden.

All around it was a high wall.

It was so high that the camel could not see over it.

But there was a gate in the wall.

The pig went through the gate.

This garden was full of fine, ripe fruit, too.

The pig ate all he wanted.

But the camel was so tall that he could not get through the gate.

"Ha, ha, ha!" laughed the pig.

"Now would you rather be tall or short?"

So the camel kept his hump, and the pig kept his snout.

For they said,
"Sometimes it's better to be tall,
And sometimes better to be small."

—*A Tale from India.*

THE LITTLE ROOSTER

I

Once there was a man who had a little rooster.

The little rooster liked to crow.

One night the man said, "How sleepy I am! I will go to bed and have a good sleep."

So he went to bed, and slept.

Next morning the little rooster got up very early and ran to the house.

He flapped his wings and crowed, "Cock-a-doodle-do!"

He crowed so loud that he waked the man.

"That must be the little rooster," said the man.

The man was so angry that he threw his hair-brush at the little rooster.

The rooster ran away as fast as he could.

Then the man said, "Now that I am up, I will plant my garden."

So he planted his garden.

That night he put the little rooster into the hen-yard.

He said, "Now I will have a long sleep."

He went to bed, and slept.

But the little rooster got up very early the next morning.

He flew out of the hen-yard and ran to the house.

"Cock-a-doodle-do!" he crowed.

The man waked up and said, "There is that little rooster again."

He was so angry that he threw his comb at the rooster.

But the little rooster had a comb. So he ran away as fast as he could.

Then the man said, "Now that I am up, I will weed my garden."

So he weeded his garden.

II

That night the man tied the little rooster in the hen-yard with a string.

He said, "Now I will have a long sleep."

So he went to bed, and slept.

The little rooster got up very early the next morning.

He bit the string in two and flew out of the hen-yard.

He ran to the house and flapped his wings.

"Cock-a-doodle-do!" he crowed.

The little rooster crowed so loud that the man waked up.

"There is that little rooster again!" said the man. "How can I sleep?"

He was as angry as he could be.

So he caught the little rooster and gave him away.

That night the man went to sleep early.

He had a long sleep.

The next night he had a long sleep.

And the next night.

And the next.

And the next.

But the weeds grew up and filled his garden.

—*Charles Battell Loomis—Adapted.*

NORTH WIND AT PLAY

I

North Wind went out one summer day.

"Now I will have a good play," he said.

He saw an apple tree full of apples.

"Oh, apple tree, come and play with me!

We can have fun together," said North Wind.

"Oh, no!" said the apple tree.

"I can not play with you. I must work.

I am helping my apples to grow.

By and by they will grow big and red.

Then little children can eat them.

Oh, no! I can not play with you."

"We will see about that," said North Wind. "I will make you play with me."

"Puff! puff!" he said, and all the apples fell to the ground.

Then North Wind saw a field of corn.

"Oh, corn, come and play with me!" he said.

"No, no, North Wind!" said the corn.

"I can not play with you just now.

I must stand still and grow.

Look under my long, green leaves.

Do you see the white grains under them?

They must grow big and yellow.

Then they can be ground at the mill.

Little children can have corn bread to eat.

No, no! I can not play with you."

"Puff! puff!" said North Wind.

All the corn fell to the ground.

II

By and by North Wind saw a lily.

"Oh, lily, come and play with me.

We can have fun together," he said.

"Oh, no, North Wind!" said the lily.

"I can not play with you today.

I must take care of my buds.

They will open soon and then they will be beautiful lilies.

Then little children will come to see me.

Oh, no! I can not play with you."

"Puff! puff!" said North Wind.

The lily hung her head.

She could not look up again.

At night North Wind went home.

"What did you do today?" said his father.

"I went out to play," said North Wind.

"But no one wanted to play with me.

So I shook the apple tree, and all the apples fell to the ground.

Then I shook the corn, and it fell, too.

I blew until the lily hung her head.

I did not want to hurt them, Father. I was only playing."

"You are too rough," said his father.

"I know you do not want to be rough.

You must stay at home in summer.

You must wait until the apples and the corn and the lilies are gone.

You may go out to play in winter.

Then you can puff all you want to."

—Old Tale.

THREE BILLY GOATS GRUFF

Once there were three billy goats.

They were all named "Gruff."

Every day they went up a hill
to eat the grass and grow fat.

They had to go over a little
brook before they came to the hill.

Over the brook was a bridge.

A Troll lived under the bridge.

He was so big and cross that
every one was afraid of him.

One day the three billy goats were going up the hill to get fat.

Little Billy Goat Gruff was the first to cross the bridge.

Trip-trap! trip-trap! went the bridge.

"Who is that tripping on my bridge?" called the Troll.

"Oh, it is just Little Billy Goat Gruff.

I am going up the hill to get fat," said the little billy goat.

"Well, I am coming to gobble you up!" said the Troll.

"Oh, no!" said Little Billy Goat.

"Do not take me! I am too little. Wait for Second Billy Goat.

He is bigger than I am."

"Well, be off with you!" said the Troll.

Soon Second Billy Goat Gruff came to the bridge.

Trip-trap! trip-trap! trip-trap! went the bridge.

"Who is that tripping on my bridge?" called the Troll.

"Oh, it is just Second Billy Goat Gruff. I am going up the hill to get fat," said the second billy goat.

"Well, I am coming to gobble you up!" said the Troll.

"Oh, no!" said Second Billy Goat. "Do not take me.

I am not very big.

Wait for Big Billy Goat.

He is bigger than I am."

"Well, be off with you!" said the Troll.

Just then Big Billy Goat
Gruff came to the bridge.

Trip-trap! trip-trap! trip-trap!
trip-trap! went the bridge.

"Who is that tripping on my
bridge?" called the Troll.

"Oh, it is just Big Billy Goat Gruff!
I am going up the hill to get fat."

"Well, I am coming to gobble you up!"
said the Troll.

"Come along, then, Troll!"
said Big Billy Goat Gruff.

So the Troll came along.

Big Billy Goat Gruff flew at him.

He caught the Troll on his horns
and threw him into the brook.

The Troll was frightened.

He jumped out of the water and ran away.

The three billy goats never saw him again.

They go up the hill every day, and now
they are as fat as they can be.

THE LITTLE PLANT

In the heart of a seed
   Buried deep, so deep,
A dear little plant
   Lay fast asleep.

"Wake!" said the sunshine,
   "And creep to the light,"
"Wake!" said the voice
   Of the raindrops bright.

The little plant heard,
   And it rose to see
What the wonderful
   Outside world might be.

—*Kate Louise Brown.*

THE SWING

How do you like to go up in a swing,
Up in the air so blue?
Oh, I do think it the pleasantest thing
Ever a child can do!

Up in the air and over the wall,
    Till I can see so wide,
Rivers and trees and cattle and all
    Over the country-side.

Till I look down on the garden green,
    Down on the roof so brown—
Up in the air I go flying again,
    Up in the air and down!

—*Robert Louis Stevenson.*

THE SLEEPING APPLE

I

A little apple hung high up on an apple tree.

It slept and grew, and slept and grew.

At last it was big and ripe, but it still slept on.

One day a little girl came walking under the tree and saw the apple.

"Why does the apple sleep so long?" said the little girl.

"The world is so beautiful!

I wish the apple would wake up and see.

Maybe I can wake it."

So she called out,

"Oh, apple, wake up! Do not sleep so long.

Wake up, wake up, and come with me!"

But the sleeping apple did not wake.

"Oh, Sun, beautiful Sun!" said the girl.

"Will you kiss the apple and make it wake? That is the way mother wakes me."

"Oh, yes," said the sun, "indeed I will."

So he kissed the apple until it was a golden yellow.

It was as golden as the sun.

But still the apple slept on.

By and by a robin flew to the tree.

"Dear Robin," said the little girl, "can you help me wake the sleeping apple?

I can not wake it, and the sun can not wake it. We have tried and tried.

It will sleep too long."

"Oh, yes, little girl, I can wake the apple," said the robin.

"I will sing to it just as I sing to my little birdies in their nest.

I wake my birdies every morning with a song."

"Cheer up! wake up! cheer up! wake up!" sang the robin in the apple tree.

But the sleeping apple did not wake.

"Oo—oo—oo—oo! Oo—oo—oo—oo!"

"Who is that coming through the trees?" said the little girl.

"Oh, it is my friend, the Wind. Oh, Wind, you wake me sometimes at night.

Can you not wake this beautiful apple?

It has slept so long."

"Indeed I can," said the wind.

"It is time for all apples to wake up.

Summer will soon be over."

"Oo—oo—oo," he said, and shook the tree.

The apple waked and fell down, down, down to the ground.

The little girl kissed its golden cheeks.

"Oh, thank you, kind wind," she said.

"If you had not come, the apple would have slept all the summer long."

—*Folk Tale.*

SWEET PORRIDGE

I

Once there was a little girl who lived with her mother.

They were very poor.

Sometimes they had no supper.

Then they went to bed hungry.

One day the little girl went into the woods.

She wanted wood for the fire.

She was so hungry and sad!

"Oh, I wish I had some sweet porridge!" she said.

"I wish I had a pot full for mother and me.

We could eat it all up."

Just then she saw an old woman with a little black pot.

She said, "Little girl, why are you so sad?"

"I am hungry," said the little girl.

"My mother is hungry, too.

We have nothing to eat.

Oh, I wish we had some sweet porridge for our supper!"

"I will help you," said the old woman.

"Take this little black pot.

When you want some sweet porridge, you must say, 'Little pot, boil!'

The little pot will boil and boil and boil.

You will have all the sweet porridge you want.

When the little pot is full, you must say, 'Little pot, stop!'

Then the little pot will stop boiling."

The little girl thanked the old woman, and ran home with the little black pot.

Then she made a fire with the wood and put the little black pot on the fire.

"Little pot, boil!" she said.

The little pot boiled and boiled and boiled, until it was full of sweet porridge.

Then the little girl said, "Little pot, stop!"

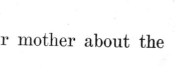

The little pot stopped boiling.

She called her mother, and they ate all the sweet porridge they wanted.

The little girl told her mother about the old woman.

"Now," they said, "we are happy.

We shall not be hungry any more."

The next day the little girl went into the woods again.

She was gone a long time.

"She will be hungry when she comes home," said her mother.

"I will boil the sweet porridge."

So she put the little black pot on the fire.

"Little pot, boil!" she said.

The little pot boiled and boiled until it was full of sweet porridge.

The mother wanted the pot to stop boiling.

But she forgot what to say.

The pot boiled and boiled.

The porridge boiled over on to the stove.

It ran all over the stove.

Then it ran all over the floor.

It flowed into the street.

It flowed on and on and on.

The people all ran out of their houses.

"Oh! Oh! Oh!" they cried.

"The sea has turned to porridge! It is flowing over the world! What shall we do?"

No one knew how to make the little black pot stop boiling.

After a long time the little girl came home. The pot was boiling and boiling.

"Little pot, stop!" said the little girl.

And the little pot stopped.

But for many days after that the street was full of sweet porridge.

When people wanted to get to the other side, they had to eat their way across.

—*Folk Tale.*

JOHNNY-CAKE

Once there were a little old man, a little old woman, and a little boy.

One day the old woman made a round Johnny-cake.

She put it into the stove to bake.

She said to the little boy, "You must bake the Johnny-cake for us.

We will eat it for supper."

Then the little old man took a spade, and the little old woman took a hoe.

They went to work in the garden.

The little boy was all alone in the house.

He forgot about the Johnny-cake.

All at once he heard a great noise.

The stove door flew open, and Johnny-cake rolled out.

Out of the house he rolled.

The little boy ran to the garden.

"Father! Mother!" he called.

Johnny-cake is rolling away."

The little old man threw down
his spade, and the little old woman
threw down her hoe.

Then they all ran as fast as
they could after Johnny-cake.

But they could not catch him.

Johnny-cake laughed and said,

"I am having some fun;
I roll and they run;
I can beat every one."

He rolled on and on.

Soon he came to a hen.

"Johnny-cake, where are you going?" asked the hen.

"Oh, I am out rolling," he said.

"I have rolled away from a little old man,

A little old woman,

A little boy,

And I can roll away from you, too-o-o-o!"

"You can, can you?" said the hen.

"We will see about that!

"I think I will just eat you up!"

So the hen ran as fast as she could.

But she could not catch Johnny-cake.

Johnny-cake laughed and said,

"I am having some fun;
I roll and they run;
I can beat every one."

He rolled on and on.

By and by he came to a cow.

"Johnny-cake, where are you going?" asked the cow.

"Oh, I am out rolling," he said.

"I have rolled away from a little old man,

A little old woman,

A little boy,

And a hen.

I can roll away from you, too-o-o-o!"

"You can, can you?" said the cow.

"I think I will just eat you up!"

The cow ran as fast as she could.

But she could not catch him.

Johnny-cake laughed and said,

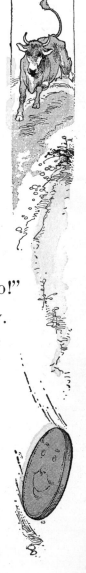

"I am having some fun;
I roll and they run;
I can beat every one."

He rolled on until he came to a pig.

The pig was lying down.

"Where are you going?" asked the pig.

"Oh, I am out rolling," said Johnny-cake.

"I have rolled away from a little old man,

A little old woman,

A little boy,

A hen,

And a cow.

I can roll away from you, too-o-o-o!"

"Woof, woof! I am sleepy," said the pig.

Johnny-cake went near to him.

"I will make you hear me!" he said.

"I have rolled away from a little old man,

A little old woman,

A little boy,

A hen,

And a cow.

I can roll away from you, too-o-o-o!"

"Woof, woof!" said the pig.

"I am sleepy. Go away!"

He shut his eyes.

Johnny-cake got as near to the pig as he could.

He shouted at him.

"Do you hear me!" he called.

"I have rolled away from

A little old man,

A little old woman,

A little boy,

A hen,

And a cow.

I can roll away from you, too-o-o-o!"

The pig opened his eyes.

He opened his mouth, too.

He caught Johnny-cake, and ate him up.

—*English Folk Tale.*

MARY AND THE LARK

Mary: Good morning, pretty lark.
Have you any birdies in that nest?

Lark: Oh, yes. I have three birdies here.
They are very beautiful, and they
are very good, too.

Mary: May I see them, pretty lark?

Lark: Oh, yes. Come here, little ones.
This is Tiny Beak, this is Light
Wing, and this is Bright Eyes.

Mary: How beautiful they are!
There are three children in our
home, too, Alice, Ned, and I.
Mother says we are very good.
We know how much she loves us.

Bright Eyes: Mother loves us, too.

Mary: I am sure she does.
Pretty lark, may I take Tiny
Beak home to play with me?

Lark: Yes, you may take Tiny Beak
home with you, if you will
bring baby Alice to us.

Mary: Oh, no, no! I can not do that.
Baby Alice can not leave mother.
She is so little!
She would not like to live out
of doors, and she is too big
for your little nest.

149

Lark: But Tiny Beak can not leave his mother.

He is such a little bird.

He is too little for your big house. He loves his little round nest the best.

Tiny Beak: Chirp, chirp, chirp! So I do!

Mary: Poor little Tiny Beak!

I will not take you.

I see that your little round nest is best for you.

Lark: North and South and East and West,

Each one loves his own home best.

Mary: Good-bye, birdies! Good-bye!

Light Wing: Good-bye, Mary!

Come to see us again soon.

THE HEN WHO WENT TO HIGH DOVER

I

Once a hen was in the woods.

When night came she flew up into an oak tree and went to sleep.

Soon she had a dream.

She dreamed that she would find a nest of golden eggs if she went to High Dover.

She waked up with a jump.

"I must go to High Dover," she said.

"I must find the nest of golden eggs."

So she flew out of the tree and went up the road.

When she had gone a little
way, she met a cock.

"Good-day, Cocky Locky!"
said the hen.

"Good-day, Henny Penny!
Where are you going so early?"
said the cock.

"I am going to High
Dover. I shall find a
nest of golden eggs
there," said the hen.

"Who told you that, Henny
Penny?" asked the cock.

"I sat in the oak tree last night
and dreamed it," said the hen.

"I will go with you." said the cock.

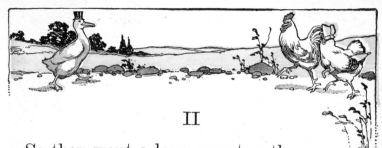

II

So they went a long way together until they met a duck.

"Good-day, Ducky Lucky!" said the cock.

"Good-day, Cocky Locky! Where are you going so early?" asked the duck.

"I am going to High Dover. I shall find a nest of golden eggs there," said the cock.

"Who told you that, Cocky Locky?" asked the duck.

"Henny Penny!" said the cock.

"Who told you that, Henny Penny?" asked the duck.

"I sat in the oak tree last night and dreamed it," said the hen.

"I will go with you!" said the duck.

So they went a long way together until they met a gander.

"Good-day, Gandy Pandy!" said the duck.

"Good-day, Ducky Lucky!" said the gander. "Where are you going so early?"

"I am going to High Dover. I shall find a nest of golden eggs there," said the duck.

"Who told you that, Ducky Lucky?" asked the gander.

"Cocky Locky!"

"Who told you that, Cocky Locky?"

"Henny Penny."

"How do you know that, Henny Penny?" asked the gander.

"I sat in the oak tree last night and dreamed it," said the hen.

"I will go with you!" said the gander.

III

So they went a long way together until they met a fox.

"Good-day, Foxy Woxy!" said the gander.

"Good-day, Gandy Pandy! Where are you going so early?" asked the fox.

"I am going to High Dover. I shall find a nest of golden eggs there," said the gander.

"Who told you that, Gandy Pandy?"

"Ducky Lucky!"

"Who told you that, Ducky Lucky?" asked the fox.

"Cocky Locky!"

"Who told you that, Cocky Locky?"

"Henny Penny!"

"How do you know that, Henny Penny?"

"I sat in the oak tree last night and dreamed it, Foxy Woxy," said the hen.

"How foolish you are!" said the fox.

"There is no nest of golden eggs at
High Dover.

You are cold and tired.

Come with me to my warm den."

So they all went with the fox to his den.

They all got warm and sleepy.

The duck and the gander went to sleep
in a corner.

But the cock and the hen slept on a roost.

IV

When they were asleep, the fox
ate the gander and the duck.

Just then the hen waked up.

She saw Cocky Locky near her.

She looked for Gandy Pandy and
Ducky Lucky.

She could not see them, but she
saw feathers on the floor!

"I must fool the fox," she said.

So she looked up the chimney.

"Oh! oh!" she called to the fox.

"Look at the geese flying by!"

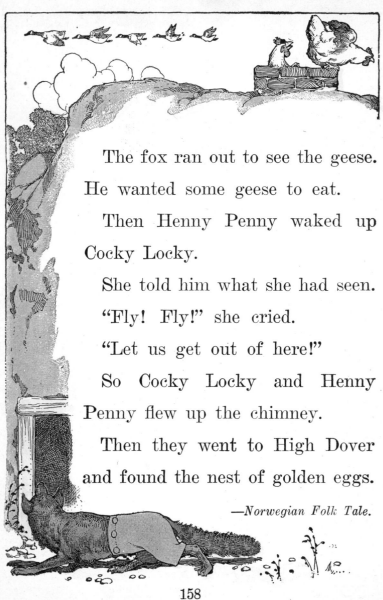

The fox ran out to see the geese.

He wanted some geese to eat.

Then Henny Penny waked up Cocky Locky.

She told him what she had seen.

"Fly! Fly!" she cried.

"Let us get out of here!"

So Cocky Locky and Henny Penny flew up the chimney.

Then they went to High Dover and found the nest of golden eggs.

—*Norwegian Folk Tale.*

158

HANSEL'S COAT

Sheep: Where is your coat, little Hansel?
It is cold this spring morning.

Hansel: I have no coat. Mother can not get
me a coat till winter comes.
I wish I could have one now.

Sheep: I will help you, Hansel.
Take some of my wool. There!
Now you can make a warm coat.

Hansel: Oh, thank you! But how can I make
a coat from this curly wool?

Thorn-bush: Come here, Hansel.
Pull the curly wool over
my long thorns. They
will comb it and make it
straight.

Hansel: Oh, thank you! How straight
and soft you have made it!
But this is not a coat yet.
What shall I do now?

Spider: Give me the wool, Hansel.
I will spin the threads, and
make them into cloth for you.
There it is.

Crab: What have you there, Hansel?

Hansel: This is cloth for a coat.

Crab: My claws are like scissors.
I will cut it out for
you. There it is!

Hansel: Thank you, kind Crab.
I wish I could sew.
Then I could make my coat.

Bird: I will sew your coat for you.
I sew my nest together
every spring. See, I
take a thread in my
beak.

Then I pull it through and through
the cloth.

There is your coat, Hansel.

Hansel: Oh, thank you all!
How happy mother will be to see my
nice warm coat. —*Folk Tale.*

THE LAMBKIN

I

Once upon a time there
was a wee, wee Lambkin.

The Lambkin
jumped about on
his little legs.

He ate the green
grass and had a fine time.

One day he thought he would go
to see his Granny.

"I shall have a fine time!" he said.

"I shall have such good things
to eat when I get there!"

The Lambkin jumped about on
his little legs.

He was as happy as he could be.

As he was going along the road he met a jackal.

Now the jackal likes to eat tender little lambkins. So the jackal said,

"Lambkin! Lambkin! I'll eat you!"

But the Lambkin jumped about on his little legs and said,

"To Granny's house I go,
Where I shall fatter grow;
Then you can eat me so."

The jackal likes fat lambs, so he let Lambkin go on to get fat.

By and by Lambkin met a tiger.

Then he met a wolf.

Then he met a dog.

They all like good things to eat.

They like tender lambkins, so they all called out,

"Lambkin! Lambkin!
We'll eat you!"

But Lambkin jumped about on his little legs and said,

"To Granny's house I go,
Where I shall fatter grow;
Then you can eat me so."

The tiger and the wolf and the dog all like fat lambkins.

So they let Lambkin go on to his Granny's to get fat.

II

At last Lambkin got to his
Granny's house. Granny came
to the door to see him.

"Oh, Granny, dear!" he said, "I have
promised to get very fat.

I must keep my promise.

Please put me into the corn-bin."

So his Granny put him into the corn-bin.

Lambkin stayed there seven days and ate
and ate and ate.

At last he grew very fat.

"How fat you are, Lambkin!" said his Granny.

"You must go home."

"Oh, no!" said Lambkin.

"The tiger might eat me up."

"But you must go home, Lambkin," said his Granny.

"Well, then," said Lambkin, "I will tell you what to do.

You must take a goat skin and make a little Drumkin. I can sit inside and roll home."

So she made a Drumkin.

Lambkin got into it, and his Granny sewed it up.

Then Lambkin began to roll along the road to his home.

166

III

Soon he met the tiger.

The tiger called out,

"Drumkin! Drumkin!

Have you seen Lambkin?"

Lambkin, in his soft nest, called back,

"Lost in the forest, and so are you!

On, little Drumkin! Tum-pa, tum-too!"

The tiger was angry. "Now I shall have

no fat Lambkin to eat," he said.

"Why didn't I eat him when I had him?"

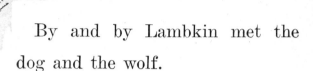

By and by Lambkin met the dog and the wolf.

They called to him,

"Drumkin! Drumkin!

Have you seen Lambkin?"

And Lambkin, in his soft, warm nest, called back to them,

"Lost in the forest, and so are you!

On, little Drumkin! Tum-pa, tum-too!"

The dog and the wolf were very angry because they had no fat Lambkin to eat.

But Lambkin rolled along laughing and singing,

"Tum-pa, tum-too!

Tum-pa, tum-too!"

At last Lambkin met the jackal, who said,

"Drumkin! Drumkin!

Have you seen Lambkin?"

Lambkin, in his soft nest, called back,

"Lost in the forest, and so are you!

On, little Drumkin! Tum-pa, tum-too!"

Now the jackal was wise. He knew Lambkin's voice. So he called out,

"Lambkin! Lambkin!

Come out of that Drumkin!"

"Come and make me!" shouted Lambkin.

The jackal ran after Drumkin.

But Drumkin rolled faster and faster, and soon rolled away from him.

The last thing the jackal heard was,

"Lost in the forest, and so are you!

On, little Drumkin! Tum-pa, tum-too!"

—A Tale from India.

SNOW-FLAKES

Child: Little white feathers
     Filling the air—
     Little white feathers!
     How came you there?

Snow-flakes: We came from the cloud-birds,
     Flying so high,
     Shaking their white wings
     Up in the sky.

Child: Little white feathers,
     Swiftly you go!
     Little white snow-flakes,
     I love you so!

Snow-flakes: We are swift because

We have work to do;

But look up at us,

And we will kiss you.

—*Mary Mapes Dodge.*

THE CLOUDS

White sheep, white sheep,

On a blue hill,

When the wind stops,

You all stand still.

You walk far away,

When the winds blow;

White sheep, white sheep,

Where do you go?

—*Old Rime.*

171

WORD LIST FOR BOOK ONE

The following list contains the words of Book One that were not taught in the Primer. Many of these words have been developed phonetically in earlier lessons, and are therefore not new to the child when read on the pages indicated. Such words are printed in italic type.

7 Gustava
spring
sun

8 more
here

9 glad
over

10 food
but
threw

11 this
yet

12 just

13 tweet-tweet
yellow
shall
if

14 such
beautiful
sony

15 hairs
never

16 soft
prettiest
ever

17 think
hung
head
hid

18 felt
very
again
as

19 cricket
bee
plan

20 place
chirp
light
try

21 sunshine
tall
buzz

22 field
fun
together

23 high
best
hiding
squeak

24 summer
many
always
great

25 every
lay
an
grew

26 please
when

27 waiting
cried
own

28 off
laughed
proud

29 Penny
first
baby
story
doggie
given

30 our
cunning
kitty-cats
creep

31 bunnies
green
leap

32 geese
duck-pond
deep

33 five
chicks

34 downy
crying

35 lullaby
closed
lambs
stars
moon
fall

36 ant
leaf
got
blew
sometime

37 catch
kept
near
bit
safe

38 cool
shade
swing
through

39 voice
below
roots
die
new
should

40 bone
across
hide

41 bridge
thought
fell
seen
shadow

42 kite
clouds
butterfly
tied
string

43 *met*
fox
fat
mice
getting

44 foolish
right

tricks
ha
better
than

45 noise
hunter
running
barking
only

46 legs
short
slow
walk
long

47 sure
worms
tree-top
shakes
hawk

48 Molly
pail
sell
money
buy
hatched

49 build

50 began
poor
counted
until

51 patter
caught
afraid

52 fine
hang
bell
neck

ting-a-ling
joy

53 wise
old
wiser
way

54 hare
tortoise
river
swim
hop
race

55 nearly
rest
before

56 slept
hopped
beats

57 flapped
called
reach

58 friend
beasts
hurt
each
talk
knew

59 stayed
well
haste
won't

60 Thanks-
giving
indeed
hungry

61 *outside*
sad
year

62 turkey
song
cut-cut-ca-
da-cut
loud

63 *wheat*

64 children
evening

65 nothing
cones

66 tired
care
shook

67 *bright*
fairy
asked

68 gold
wonderful

69 stocking
darling
write
corner
Santa
goodies
toe

70 country
men

71 Abraham
Lincoln

173

72 flags
hue

73 stripes

74 window
parade
George
Washington
birthday

75 last

76 street
told

77 grain
plant
grow
ripe

78 reap
thresh

79 flour
bake
loaf

81 Brownie
why
ten
breaking
nine

82 six
seven
eight

83 *hark*
·

84 goats
grass
turnip

85 because

86 wolf

88 sea
wide
fish
swam

89 cranes
strong
beaks

91 held
claws
fatter

92 robins
reason
lark

93 Jenny Wren
I'm
chick-a-dee

94 does
birdie
longer
till
stronger
flies

95 rise
limbs

96 oak
acorns
tried

97 *hit* ·
woman
cloth

98 baker
forest

101 pine
needles

102 glass

103 broke

105 gosling
learn
duckling
quack

106 colt

107 calf

108 *gate*
open

109 world
mule
pulling

110 frightened
shouted

112 camel
hump
snout

113 *wall*
fruit

114 *inside*
rather
or

115 it's
small

116 rooster
crow
early
angry
hair-brush

117 comb

118 weed

120 work
puff

121 *stand*

122 lily
buds
lilies

123 rough
gone

124 billy
Gruff
Troll

125 trip-trap
tripping
gobble
second
bigger

129 heart
seed
buried
raindrops
rose
might

130 air
pleasantest
child

131 cattle
roof

133 kiss
golden

135 cheeks

174

136 supper
    fire
    sweet
    porridge
    pot
137 boil

140 stove
    flowed
    people
    turned

142 Johny-cake
    spade
    hoe
    door
    rolled

143 having

146 lying
    woof

148 Mary
    Tiny
149 much
150 South
    East
    West
151 dream
    High Dover
152 Cocky
    Locky
    Henny
    Penny
153 Ducky
    Lucky
154 gander
    Gandy
    Pandy
155 Foxy Woxy
156 *den*

157 feathers
    chimney

159 Hansel
    curly

160 thorns
    straight
    spin
    threads

161 scissors
    crab
    sew

162 Lambkin
    Granny

163 jackal
    tender
    I'll

164 tiger
    we'll

165 promised
    corn-bin

166 skin
    Drumkin

167 tum-pa,
    tum-too
    didn't

169 faster

170 shaking
    sky
    swiftly
    snow-flakes